Evi, My Little Monkey

Neithard Horn

4880 Lower Valley Road, Atglen, PA 19310

Painted for my daughter Eva.
Wien 1978, Darmstadt 1987

Copyright © 2011 by Neithard Horn

Library of Congress Control Number: 2011927106

Type set in Lucida Bright

ISBN: 978-0-7643-3827-4
Printed in China

Schiffer Books are available at special discounts for bulk purchases for sales promotions or premiums. Special editions, including personalized covers, corporate imprints, and excerpts can be created in large quantities for special needs. For more information contact the publisher:

Published by Schiffer Publishing Ltd.
4880 Lower Valley Road
Atglen, PA 19310
Phone: (610) 593-1777; Fax: (610) 593-2002
E-mail: Info@schifferbooks.com

For the largest selection of fine reference books on this and related subjects, please visit our website at **www.schifferbooks.com**
We are always looking for people to write books on new and related subjects. If you have an idea for a book please contact us at the above address.

This book may be purchased from the publisher.
Include $5.00 for shipping.
Please try your bookstore first.
You may write for a free catalog.

In Europe, Schiffer books are distributed by
Bushwood Books
6 Marksbury Ave.
Kew Gardens
Surrey TW9 4JF England
Phone: 44 (0) 20 8392 8585;
Fax: 44 (0) 20 8392 9876
E-mail: info@bushwoodbooks.co.uk
Website: www.bushwoodbooks.co.uk

Neithard Horn

Evi, My Little Monkey

A Good Night Book for You
and for Grown-ups, Too

For: _____

From: _____

here it is evening
there it is tomorrow
but maybe
you will meet EviMonkey
in a dream
in a far away land

when the sun goes to sleep
and the moon rises behind the trees
Evi, my little monkey, wakes up

necessities of life

bananas and a coconut for EviMonkey

EviMonkey goes for a walk

EviMonkey
visits the moon

EviMonkey plays in the trees

EviMonkey
builds a tower

EviMonkey paints a picture

EviMonkey meets the Gods

reflections and illusions
for EviMonkey

EviMonkey thinks about something

the moon disappears behind the trees
and EviMonkey is tired

sleep well, Evi, my little monkey,
and dream a beautiful dream

This is the end of the book.
But tomorrow is another day,
maybe we'll look at it again.

And later, when you go to sleep
EviMonkey wakes up again
and then
maybe you'll play together
in your sleep
in a dream
in a land far away from here

About the Author

The complete Book, title and contents, style, mood, colors, materials, and techniques, even the message and the intent, appeared like in a Flash at the same instant in front of the eyes of my mind and stayed there; it was like gazing into a multi-faceted crystal which I could turn at will, each facet a page or a frame of the Book, complete with captions, which later I could recall in detail any time any place.

That happened to me two weeks into a retreat in Vienna, Austria, where I focused on what was in front of me. I was into the fourth hour of a hard-core training session.

FlashBang! And there it was, out of nowhere, as it seemed to me, although I knew that the whole idea had it's roots in my past. Now I didn't focus on what was in front of me anymore but on the crystal in my mind, turning it this way and that, constructing the Book in my head. Then I stood up and left the training sessions.

Since at that time I was living in an old part of Vienna, I had all the necessities of an undisturbed life—drink, food, and safe shelter, and since I began to take myself more seriously as an artist—and following an inspiration come hell or bad weather was part of my whole artist-idea—I organized a stack of paper, pencil and eraser, pen and ink, colored pencils, and set down to work and painted the Book I saw in my mind. After about six months the work was done, I was quite pleased with it, but other pressing matters of my restless life forced me to put it in my portfolio, and then I forgot about it.

About seven years later it came to pass that I lived in Darmstadt (a medium-sized residential city in central Germany with a conservative, artistic-minded population) as a known and accepted off-the-mainstream artist, drawing and painting full time and then some, having shows and newspaper snippets, and generally playing the art-scene-game, enjoying my life as an artist very much, in spite of all hardships.

One day I browsed through my archive and found the Book I had painted years ago in Vienna, and I looked at it like new, and I decided to paint it once more. I still liked it a lot, but since those days I had learned more about my art and more about contemporary comic- and cartoon-art, and in comparison I didn't find my artwork good enough anymore.

Since I had—courtesy of the City of Darmstadt—drink, food, and safe shelter, I organized a stack of paper (this time bigger, ordered in double-page spreads, and in different textures), pencil and eraser, pen and ink, brushes and aquarelle-colors, which had become my most beloved medium.

Then I sat down to work and about 10 months later the work was done, this Book as you hold it in your hands—the Vienna version streamlined and polished, a few pages and frames added, a few episodes elaborated due to my then expanded awareness. The Book was ready to be published worldwide because I laid out special frames for the captions where the words could easily be changed into another language and script. Working on it I had dedicated the Book to all children on planet earth, even if I was then, and am now, aware that too many children have too many difficulties to survive let alone enjoy a beautiful children's book.

Since I am a book person, I want to introduce books to children as early as possible, and I have always wanted a book that I myself wouldn't get bored with while looking at it with a child, but it still needed to be within a child's understanding and a little above to keep them interested. And the art work must be intricate enough to satisfy the most discerning adult so he/she doesn't get bored while the child keeps looking and talking. After searching for quite a long time I decided that I'd would have to paint it myself —which years later I did.

Naturally I have my own educational agenda with the Book—one that is valid for both the child and the grown-up—which is: To find the logical order of the frames on a page or double page spread; to learn how to tell a story along a narrative given only in pictures, and what goes on between the pictures, with the spoken word (maybe later with the written word as little essays); to talk about what the pictures can't show; to learn how to verbally describe, and later interpret, a visual impression; and to use the captions to teach reading. Simultaneously I am trying to influence the child's sense of harmony and beauty as I, as a responsible adult, think fit.

So, this book is a PICTURE-book, not a WORD-book. The pictures tell the story—actually you tell the story to yourself as you look at the pictures and connect them with each other trying to figure out what's going on. The captions are written only to send your imagination along the right track.

Each spread is a mosaic and the parts of the mosaic and the flow of the story are not always ordered top-left to bottom-right like in a word-book, because maybe the other way around makes more visual sense, and for a child it doesn't really matter anyway.

It took me almost a year to paint the book and I enjoyed every second of it and I sincerely hope you enjoy it just as much...

...and mistake me not—even if I say so myself: This book is a work of art coming at you in the disguise of a children's book.